Once Upon an Everyday

C151635673

For Jean – T.F

ONCE UPON AN EVERYDAY
A PICTURE CORGI BOOK : 0 552 546216

First published in Great Britain by Doubleday, a division of
Transworld Publishers

PRINTING HISTORY
Doubleday edition published 2000
Picture Corgi edition published 2001

1 3 5 7 9 10 8 6 4 2

Text copyright © Toby Forward, 2000
Illustrations copyright © Sophy Williams, 2000

Designed by Tracey Hurst

The right of Toby Forward to be identified as the author and of
Sophy Williams as the illustrator of this work has been asserted in
accordance with the Copyright, Designs and Patents Act 1988

Condition of sale
This book is sold subject to the condition that it shall not, by way of
trade or otherwise, be lent, re-sold, hired out or otherwise circulated
without the publisher's prior consent in any form of binding or cover
other than that in which it is published and without a similar condition
including this condition being imposed on the subsequent purchaser.

Picture Corgi Books are published by Transworld Publishers,
61-63 Uxbridge Road, London W5 5SA,
a division of The Random House Group Ltd,
in Australia by Random House Australia (Pty) Ltd,
20 Alfred Street, Milsons Point, Sydney, NSW 2061,
in New Zealand by Random House New Zealand Ltd,
18 Poland Road, Glenfield, Auckland 10,
and in South Africa by Random House (Pty) Ltd,
Endulini, 5A Jubilee Road, Parktown 2193

Printed in Singapore

www.booksattransworld.co.uk/childrens

KENT
ARTS & LIBRARIES
C151635673

CF

Once Upon an Everyday

Toby Forward

Illustrated by Sophy Williams

PICTURE CORGI BOOKS

I have never gone to sea in a pirate ship, or worn a golden ring in my ear, or had a parrot on my shoulder, or dug up hidden treasure from a secret map where X marks the spot.

But I once went fishing with a net,
and I didn't catch a single fish,

but I found a frog, as green as grass and wet as soap,

and I tried to pick him up but he
slithered through my fingers and splashed
into the pool.

I have never chased a ghost along a haunted passageway or seen bats spread leather wings and flap through cobwebs while owls hoot.

But I once walked my
grandma to the shops all on my own,

and I was so careful when we
crossed the road,

and she bought me a glass of milk and
a cake in the big store.

I have never run away from home to
join the circus, or painted my face like a clown,
or driven in a car that falls to pieces
or squirted water at my sister.

But I once stood close to a bonfire, as hot as holidays and as big as a house,

and I saw the rockets
burst above me in the
autumn sky and I heard
the thundercracks,

and I watched the coloured sparks
pour down like painted fountains,
and smelled the smoke and tasted
the explosions.

I have never run with wolves through forests, or climbed with bears in woods that hang above your head like arms stretched up, or seen the moon ride through the night.

But I once camped in the garden
in a tent,

and Dad slept next to me.

He was startled when a rabbit woke us up
and he thought he was in bed,

but we laughed and went back
to sleep.

I have never breathed the smoke
from a dragon's mouth, or seen his silver
scales, or heard his claws scrape on the grey
stone floor of a gloomy cave, or cut the ropes
that held his prisoner and watched the dragon
circle overhead.

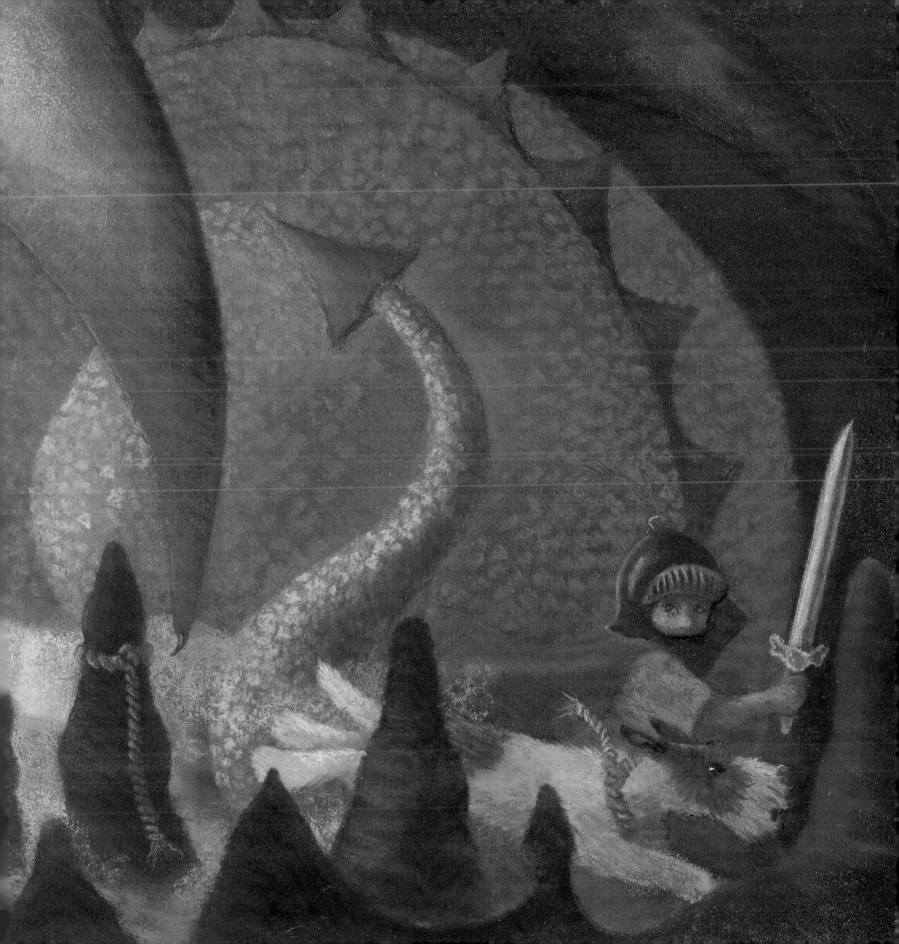

Βut I once made my mum a
ring out of silver paper

and the smoothest button of glass, as
red as lips and clear as day,

and she wore it to a party.

I have never surfed the ocean on a board and looked down through the rippling water to the world below and seen the jellyfish with streaming fronds, or swum with dolphins, or heard the whales calling to each other through the deep.

But I once picked up my little brother,

and he held my finger tight as tight
in his tiny fist

and I rocked him gently and I sang to him.
I made him go to sleep when nobody else could do it.